# Roots, Research & Reflections:

## *One Woman's History in the Making*

Ruth Ann Butler

*To: Donald Wright*
*Thanks for your support.*

*Ruth A. Butler*
*7/14/2017*

INTRODUCTION

PERSONAL REFLECTION

CHAPTER 1: AN AFTERTHOUGHT

CHAPTER 2: SOLID ROOTS

CHAPTER 3: STERLING MEMORIES

CHAPTER 4: CALL FOR HIGHER LEARNING

CHAPTER 5: UNEXPECTED GUEST

CHAPTER 6: IT RUNS IN THE FAMILY

CHAPTER 7: STAYING POWER

CHAPTER 8: HISTORY IN THE MAKING

CHAPTER 9: TROUBLED TIMES AHEAD

CHAPTER 10: A VERY SPECIAL REUNION

CHAPTER 11: WOMEN MAKING HISTORY

CHAPTER 12: RESEARCH & RECONCILIATION

CHAPTER 13: RICHLAND CEMETERY

CHAPTER 14: THE GIFT OF RESEARCH

ACKNOWLEDGEMENTS

ABOUT THE AUTHOR

# DEDICATION

This book is dedicated to anyone struggling with a disability: You are an overcomer. You can achieve whatever the Lord so designed you to achieve.

"May HE grant you your heart's desires and fulfill all of your plans."....**Psalm 20:4**

This book is also dedicated to my Aunt Virginia Butler Coker who encouraged me to write and share my story. Thanks Aunt "Gin".

*---Ruth Ann Butler*

## INTRODUCTION:

 In so many ways, Ruth Ann Butler is a fearless fighter. She grew up in a textile town in the segregated South with a physical disability that kept her from doing many things other children her age could do. She faced many personal challenges—one involved putting her newborn son up for adoption—in an era when single mothers faced overwhelming social bias and daunting job prospects. That was the most heart-wrenching decision she ever made.

But Ruth Ann doesn't dwell on the negative or what could have been. She overcomes and moves forward. She overcame financial hurdles when pursuing her college education and when establishing the Upstate's only black history museum. Through genealogy and historical research, she looks to the past for support, pride and direction for the future.

In Greenville, SC, it's hard to find anyone in the city's leadership or community service fields who doesn't know Ruth Ann Butler. She was born and bred in the city and her name is calling card enough when she gathers support for any of her projects. That wasn't always the case as she has worked tirelessly over the years to build a solid rapport with the community she has so loyally served.

At 73, Butler balances *many* hats. She is a retired educator, local history and genealogy buff, research enthusiast, consultant, civil rights activist, museum curator, businesswoman, writer, author, avid storyteller, public speaker, community volunteer, an authority on African-American history in Upstate South Carolina and a devoted member of Allen Temple AME Church. She is also a loving

sister, aunt, and proud mother of one son and grandmother of two.

She founded the Greenville Cultural Exchange Center more than 29 years ago. The center has been an invaluable hub for information and activity surrounding black history in South Carolina.

The renovated two-story house on Arlington Avenue is just a few minutes from Downtown Greenville. It houses a treasure of artifacts, photographs and publications documenting the struggles and achievements of African-Americans.

More than a decade ago, Butler launched the annual Women Making History Awards, which honors local women who have positively impacted the community in business, education, the arts, social and community services.

She has initiated and overseen numerous research and genealogy projects for Greenville County as well as for the City of Greenville. Butler was the first black member of the Greenville Chapter of The South Carolina Genealogical Society. She served on the board for the Greenville County Library System for 12 years.

She has been featured in The Greenville News, TOWN magazine, USA Today, TALK magazine and numerous other publications. Most recently, she was featured in the book, "Legendary Locals of Greenville" by local journalist and author Cindy Landrum.

"I'm so privileged to have known her for many years," said Judith Prince, Director of Academic Engagement at University of South Carolina Upstate. Prince who has worked with Butler on the Women Making History Awards and the Leadership Greenville program, said Butler is a gift to the community.

As executive director for the Greenville Cultural Exchange Center, Butler doesn't receive a paycheck. "She has overcome so many obstacles and has kept the center going," Prince said. "Her knowledge of history is just incredible and she just gives and gives, not seeking recognition."

Ginny Stroud, community development administrator for the City of Greenville, said the city has benefited greatly from Butler's efforts and expertise.

The city provided approximately $20,000 for help with renovation and repairs, Stroud said.

"I think it's important that we understand the role that African Americans have played in the history of Greenville," Stroud said. The center has helped to establish a voice to be heard for generations to come. "Ruth Ann has a wonderful collection of items she is willing to share with individuals and groups," she said.

Butler also conducts genealogy workshops for the Greenville County Library System and does research on historically black neighborhoods in the Greenville area. "Her research is very comprehensive and thorough," Stroud said.

In June 2014, the city created a Neighborhood Vibrancy Task Force designed to develop historic profiles for several African-American neighborhoods and study ways to revitalize these areas, Stroud said. The target communities are: Greenline/Spartanburg, West Greenville, Southernside, Pleasant Valley and Nicholtown.

"Ruth Ann has been a valuable resource on the five neighborhoods we've been studying," Stroud said. "Just sitting down and talking to her is a real treat. She's a wonderful speaker, very engrossing and just captures your attention."

Local businessman Joe Erwin said he knew Ruth Ann was a special person from the moment they met. Erwin is co-founder of Erwin Penland and is past Honorary Chairperson for the Women Making History Awards.

Erwin vividly recalled meeting Ruth Ann for the first time. It was in the late '80s. He was heading a small but growing advertising company. Staff just moved their office from humble beginnings on South Pleasantburg Drive to a bigger and better presence—at the corner of Falls and Broad Streets in Downtown Greenville.

"This was about two years after we founded the company," Erwin said. "And after a lot of searching for office space...I was really enthused about the potential of moving into this historical building."

Erected in the 1920s, the building was once home to several black businesses in Greenville. It was also a cultural hub for the city's prominent African-American leaders.

"I knew a little about the history of the building and its importance in the black community," he said. "But I didn't know a ton about it."

Ruth Ann, however, made sure Erwin got a history lesson he would never forget. One day, she waltzed into the lobby and walked to the reception desk stating that she needed to speak with Mr. Joe Erwin.

"So they come and get me. Here is this woman standing there whom I never met before," Erwin said recalling her bold but respectful demeanor.

"She said, 'I want to talk to you about this building.' ... She just looked me right in the eye and said, 'Mr. Erwin, you shouldn't be allowed to own this building.'"

A young, wide-eyed entrepreneur at the time, Erwin was a bit confused and taken aback. "I didn't know what to make of it....So I looked at her and I said, 'Please explain.'"

*This building was once known as the Working Benevolent Temple and Professional Building and housed several black prominent businesses. Today, it still stands at the corner of Falls and Broad Streets and is home to Erwin Penland Advertising in burgeoning Downtown Greenville. The building is listed on the National Register of Historic Places.*

And so she did as only Ruth Ann could do. She went into detail about the historical significance of the building and how it was a business and social pinnacle for Greenville's black community. She explained how segregation prevented blacks from owning and operating businesses on Main Street.

"But in this building, just a block off Main, there were retail shops owned by black Greenville residents," Erwin said. There were also offices owned by a doctor, dentist and lawyer. One floor was even reserved for parties and other social events.

After their conversation, it became clear to Erwin that Ruth Ann's insight and knowledge was not to be taken lightly.

"She was obviously someone of stature here in Greenville." But she wasn't haughty about her mission. It was her passion and compassion that impressed Erwin the most.

"She just wanted it to be understood that the building should be owned by everyone in Greenville because it was such an icon for the black community."

Erwin said since then, he and others carry a deeper appreciation of what that building means to the community from a historical and emotional standpoint.

Years later, when Erwin Penland outgrew the building, the company made a conscious decision to expand in a way that would complement the legacy of the original edifice.

"We knew we were going to need a second building... We didn't want to design something that would be all glass and steel or in the shape of a pyramid," Erwin said. "Although we were an ad agency and agencies tend to express themselves sometimes dramatically, we did not want to do anything architecturally in any way that would overwhelm the original building."

Formerly known as the Working Benevolent Temple and Professional Building, it is listed on the National Register of Historic Places. According to the South Carolina Department of Archives and History website, it was built in 1922, housed the first black mortuary in Greenville and was the center for the city's civil rights activities during the 1960s.

The entire Greenville community benefits from Ruth Ann's work, skills and knowledge. "She is one of those people in this community that others need to know how important she is," Erwin said.

Butler taught in the public schools in Georgia and South Carolina for 18 years, worked for the Legal Services Agency of Western Carolina, Neighborhoods in Action, the Appalachian Council of Governments and has done research for Allen Temple AME Church which is now listed on the National Register of Historic Places. She currently serves on the Greenville County Historic Preservation Commission.

Butler was a research consultant for a PBS documentary about the famed Fountain Inn tap dancer Peg Leg Bates, a consultant for three books on the life of the Rev. Jesse L. Jackson and for the South Carolina African American History Calendar presented by Bell South. Butler is the recipient of numerous awards including a leadership award from the local Phillis Wheatley Association.

"Ruth Ann is a loving person. She is dedicated to helping others," said Linda Sullivan, a long-time friend and retired administrator in Mauldin. Sullivan first met Butler at Bryson High School in Fountain Inn where she was a senior and Butler was a teacher. *(Bryson was one of four high schools serving the Greenville County's black population. The high school ceased to exist in 1970 after the United States Supreme Court ordered that all public schools be desegregated) Source:*

While Sullivan was not in any of Butler's classes, they still spoke to each other on campus. Sullivan remembered Butler as very friendly and approachable. "She had a way with students," Sullivan said. "I could feel her warmth. She didn't talk down to us."

More than 20 years later, they crossed paths again at Legal Services Agency of Western Carolina, a law firm that served the poor. Sullivan was a legal secretary for the agency while Butler worked with the VISTA program. Judge Robert Jenkins, who was CEO of the agency at the time, hired Butler.

Once you've become Ruth Ann's friend, you stay her friend, said Sullivan, who has served on the board for the Greenville Cultural Exchange Center and on the committee for the Women Making History Awards.

Butler has gone through a lot of ups and downs operating the center but she's persevered. "She has friends and a lot of faith. She's not a quitter," Sullivan said adding that Ruth Ann works tirelessly at the center doing research and documenting history. "She will always push forward."


*****


After decades of researching and telling other people's stories, Butler has finally decided to share her own.

---*Margaret Rose Media LLC*

## Personal Reflection:

If anybody would have told me when I was growing up that I would have ended up being an author, teacher and directing a museum, I would have said, "No way!"

I had no idea I would have ended up doing what I did. Sometimes it just blows my mind. I was totally withdrawn as a child in part because of my disability. I've learned a lot from a lot of people.

For instance, I've learned how to conduct business from my grandfather, Columbus Hood. He lived to be 99 years. He was a wise man. He told me to carefully read documents before you sign them and to get copies of them.

If you can't see the fine print, get a magnifying glass, he said. And if you don't understand something, ask questions. It made a difference when I bought my first car, a house and when I purchased the Greenville Cultural Exchange Center.

I learned to treat everybody right from my dad. He said when you climb that ladder of success, you never know when you will need those you pass along the way.

I can go on and on with valued advice I've acquired over the years.

The fact is we are all standing on somebody else's shoulders. We just didn't get where we are by ourselves. I know I'm standing on some shoulders. That's why I don't mind helping others, especially the younger generation.

I also emphasize in my talks that success is not always about making money. Money is necessary but it's not everything. It should not define who you are or your legacy. Integrity, growth, maturity and compassion are priceless assets.

It has been an amazing journey and quite humbling. As I reflect on my journey, one of my favorite Bible verses comes to mind:

"I can do all things through Christ who strengthens me." (Philippians 4:13)

My philosophy is this: listen, trust and obey God and use the talents that the Lord has given you and He will bless you because He is faithful.

I've always tried to look beyond my circumstances while trusting the Lord so that He will enable me to do whatever it is I need to do to live out His perfect will.

Just like the next person, I've had my share of struggles, ups and downs. For instance, the city shut the doors to the Greenville Cultural Exchange Center once due to building code issues. I've also been burned by people whom I thought I could trust but who only wanted to drain my resources for their personal gain. I won't name specific parties, but I will say that through it all, my God has never failed me.

Another favorite verse of mine is Romans 8:28: "And we know that in all things God works for the good of those who love him, who have been called according to His purpose."

I know the Lord called me to do the work that I'm doing.

He has never failed me in helping me to overcome financial, emotional and physical challenges. Through it all, the Lord's grace and mercy has kept me. I'm so grateful and humbled that I can reflect and share my story with others.

Here is my testimony..................

## Chapter 1: An Afterthought

I dress myself using one hand. I drive with one hand. I type on the computer with one hand. I cook and turn pages of a book the same way. Even though I was born with a birth defect that affected the entire left side of my body, I never really considered myself "handicapped."

I was diagnosed with cerebral spastic infantile paralysis. (Now, there's a mouthful.) I had (and still have) very limited use of muscles on my left side. In the beginning, even walking was a challenge. One side of my body was two sizes larger than the

*Here's a picture of me as a child prior to having surgery on my left arm which I held at a 90 degree angle. To rectify my paralysis, doctors released a bone to increase mobility. Prior to fourth grade, I was a totally withdrawn child.*

other and each foot required a different shoe size. My left elbow was held up at a 90 degree angle.

Doctors operated on my left arm and released a bone so that I could bring my arm down by my side.

But like I said, I didn't consider myself "handicapped." I just did things differently.

I believe I carried myself in such a way that some folks didn't initially notice and never gave it a second thought. I didn't want them to either. I was determined to be as independent as possible.

Life is never a cakewalk, of course, regardless of your circumstances. So for me, growing up, there were challenges. I dare the average person who is not disabled to try and dress themselves, or put on jewelry or balance a food tray on your lap while eating off of it—using one hand. Not easy.

Nevertheless, through the grace of God, I continued to get around those everyday tasks—tasks that so many folks take for granted. Instead of getting shoes from your average store, I got mine from Shriners Hospital until I reached the eighth grade. The hospital had a room full of shoes where I could pick out any style I wanted and then get the size I needed.

I was wearing a size five for my left foot and a size seven for my right foot for a long time. My overall mobility did improve. I eventually progressed to the point where I began wearing the same shoe size for both feet in the ninth grade.

My body was never balanced. There were two things I always wanted to learn but didn't. That's play the piano and ride a bicycle.

As a little child, I often ditched an active playground to avoid naturally curious children who would ask me about my walk and appearance. My doctor advised against it anyway. My left eye was very weak so if I played and became overly active, I could wind up cross eyed.

I could not swing from the monkey bars or ride a bicycle because one leg was shorter than the other. Instead, I played marbles and jackstone. Sometimes, I just sat by myself, totally withdrawn.

I had no control of my diagnosis, but I wasn't about to develop a handicapped mentality. I had to come to terms with my situation.

The playground is a lot like life, no matter your age. There are many things to explore. Some areas become favorites. Other things we want to tackle just for the fun of it.

I may not have been able to dangle from the monkey bars like other children but I could play marbles, checkers, jackstones, horseshoes and even some hopscotch.

I attended Nicholtown Elementary School on Palm Street from second through the eighth grade. (Back then, there wasn't junior high or middle school. It was elementary and high school.) I recall Nicholtown Elementary not having a sufficient heating system but teachers, staff and students worked around setbacks. For instance, when it got cold, classes would be held in the cafeteria.

The summer before I entered fourth grade, I had surgery on my arm.

My fourth grade teacher, Minnesota Gilliam, had a profound impact on how I saw myself. She said, "When you accept your handicap, everybody will accept it also." That advice has stuck with me ever since.

*Minnesota Gilliam was Ruth Ann Butler's fourth grade teacher at Nicholtown Elementary. She was one of the many positive influences in Ruth Ann's life and encouraged her to think and act beyond her disability.*

## Chapter 2: Solid Roots

I was born Christmas Day, Dec. 25, 1943 at approximately 10:00 p.m. and delivered by a midwife, Elizabeth (Lizzie) Johnson. I was born into a wonderful, loving family. I had a positive upbringing. I was the ninth child of 10 children. My parents were The Rev. Clarence Edward (C.E.) and Nina Westfield Butler.

When daddy first laid eyes on mom, he was determined that she would be his wife. He lived in Brutontown community and she lived on Hampton Avenue. They met at school and when my dad saw my mom, Cupid struck him – hard.

He later found out that my mom was a member of Tabernacle Baptist Church. He became a regular visitor there and then a member.

My parents got married in 1930 in the pastor's study at Springfield Baptist Church. The Rev. C.F. Gandy conducted our ceremony, the same day he celebrated his own 25th wedding anniversary.

My parents' marriage was a solid 45-year union. Their influence was such a blessing. My father died January 27, 1975 and my mother passed Feb. 5, 1991.

My father balanced raising a large family and working at Shriners Hospital. He also pastored five different Baptist churches during his lifetime: Jubilee Baptist Church in Taylors, one of the oldest black churches in Greenville; Mount Ararat Baptist Church in Travelers Rest; Mount Sinai Baptist Church in Travelers Rest; Bethlehem Baptist Church in Simpsonville; and Friendship Baptist Church in Greenville where he eventually became a full-time pastor during the '60's.

Occasionally, he would preach at his home church, Tabernacle Baptist on Hudson Street in Greenville.

My dad was also a skilled auto mechanic, gardener and handyman. He repaired watches on the side, painted, did carpentry and brick masonry. It didn't stop there, amazingly so. My dad was gifted in the arts. He could cook, sew, loved to sing and play the piano. He was also a huge sports fan, enjoyed fishing and developed his own baseball pitch he called the "dusty mule."

I was raised in the historic Nicholtown community on Ackley Road. (White folks lived along half of the road while blacks lived on the other, and the part of the road where blacks resided was not paved.)

*Ruth Ann Butler's mom, Mrs. Nina Westfield, wore many hats. She was a minister's wife, mom, cook, housekeeper, Girl Scout Leader, community volunteer and a mother figure to other children in the neighborhood.*

Rev. C. E. & Nina Westfield Butler

*Ruth Ann Butler's parents raised their children in a loving and disciplined home. Her dad, Rev. Clarence Edward (C.E.) Butler was also a talented carpenter, watch repairman and mechanic.*

*Ruth Ann Butler's parents standing in the living room in their house on Ackley Road celebrating their wedding anniversary.*

*This is the desk where Rev. C.E. Butler repaired watches.*

9

*John Henry & Maybelle Butler, my*
*grandparents on my father's side*

*My grandmother and my mother's stepdad: Columbus & Willie Hall Hood*

*Great grandmother Ella Anderson Hall Talley with a young Nina Westfield Butler*

*Maybelle Butler, wife of John Henry Butler*

*Butler Family photo: Top (from left to right): Willie Charles, Ruth Ann, Horace L., Clarence Jr., T.C., Grady and James Curtis Bottom (from left to right): C.E. Butler, Nina Jean Lewis, Louella, Mrs. Nina and Maybelle Randolph*

*Ruth Ann Butler on the front lawn of her house on Ackley Road in Nicholtown*

*The Butler Boys in the 1930's: Ruth Ann Butler's three oldest brothers (from left to right): Willie Charles, Clarence Jr and Grady*

Back then, many of the lots were open corn fields in the community. Those who lived in homes owned them and took pride in their properties.

We had a functional and quaint one-story home with a total of four rooms. We had roll-away beds and an outhouse. Over the years, daddy built additional rooms, including three bathrooms.

Our front yard boasted a lovely array of flowers, and in the backyard we had a vegetable garden with rows that reaped okra, corn, sweet potato and other hearty vegetables. We also had chickens, hogs, a rabbit, dog, kittens and a cow named "Bell."

My mother was a dedicated, skillful and resourceful homemaker who cared for other children in the community as well as for her own. She was also a Girl Scout leader at Friendship Baptist Church for several years. We had one of the largest troops in the district.

When I was older, I drove my mother to the meetings because she never drove. I was a teacher at the time so while my mom conducted her meeting, I sat off somewhere grading papers. That detachment didn't last long.

I soon found myself more involved as mom took advantage of my presence, asking for my assistance with troop activities. At the time, I was just mom's ride. I didn't expect to become a Girl Scout leader but that's what happened.

I eventually received leadership training. I was a Girl Scout leader for 12 years and found myself more physically active with my troops than when I was a child.

I played ball, jumped rope and camped outside. In a way, I lived out my childhood through the Girl Scouts and it was fun!

You can say it was an unexpected recruitment, courtesy of my mother—dedicated troop leader. My mom was the epitome of classy femininity. She was a poised pastor's wife: prim, proper, donning stylish hats and modest dresses. She often wore her long, wavy hair in a bun using all sorts of ornate hair pins.

At the same time, she was a hard worker and knew how to roll up her sleeves when necessary. She could be assertive and downright sassy when she wanted to.

She didn't work outside the home but her efforts at home and in the community were no less valuable. Many children in the neighborhood ended up in our yard. They called her "Mrs. Nina." She provided lemonade and cookies for all of us.

My mom had two rules: no arguing or fighting. If we were caught doing either, our playing privileges were immediately taken away. That meant no baseball, basketball, horseshoes and other toys.

It was called home training. Back then, parents meant what they said and children took heed and were very aware of the consequences if they didn't obey.

My mom would instruct us on how to behave when we had guests at home or when we would attend church or would travel elsewhere in public.

She was a true disciplinarian—loving, but stern and consistent.

If we were misbehaving and not doing what we were supposed to do, all she had to do was give us "the look" and we knew we were going to get it when we got home.

Family values were very important for my parents.

Quality time with family, especially during the holidays was a priority even when we were all grown up and moved out.

Every year, the family gathered together for Thanksgiving dinner at 310 Ackley Road—no ifs, ands or buts.

My brother Horace, initiated another tradition. He began hosting a family time for exchanging gifts.

This led to my siblings taking turns to host family Christmas dinner at their homes. I will always cherish those memories filled with the three "Fs": family, food and fun.

There were many stresses and challenges, especially for a black family growing up in the segregated South. Our access to public facilities like restrooms and restaurants were limited. If we were allowed to buy food at a white-owned restaurant, we could not sit down and eat there.

Blacks were not allowed to try on clothes in stores before we purchased them. Job opportunities were abysmal. Many were limited to low-paying housekeeping and janitorial positions. And when nightfall came, blacks were expected to remain within the boundaries of their communities.

One benefit to this was that many black communities were self-sufficient. For instance, Nicholtown had its own grocery store, a seamstress and a local plumber and everybody grew a lot of their own food.

Thankfully, our parents provided a loving, disciplined and safe environment at home. Our parents walked the Christian talk and led by example. They have passed away as well as six of my siblings.

No individual or family is perfect of course, but I consider myself extremely blessed to have been raised with such strong family ties and a solid sense of belonging and place.

*Pictured above: Maybelle, Mrs. Nina, Nina Jean, Louella and Ruth Ann*

*Although I was part of a large family, love was never lost. My siblings and I were always close and looked out for each other.*

John Richardson, a white man who lived on Piedmont Highway, was the father of my mother. My grandmother, Willie Hall, worked for Richardson and had a baby from Richardson. I later connected with Richardson's relatives after I reached out to my cousin Lillian Gilreath. Gilreath is the granddaughter of Mary Richardson, John's sister.

My grandfather, John Richardson died in 1916. It was Oct. 12, the same day my mom was born.

## Chapter 3: Sterling Memories

Call me a geek but I loved school! I was an above average student who enjoyed math and community service and wanted to be a social worker. I relished learning and saw education as a powerful tool to broaden my horizons. I loved reading. There was a public library on McBee Avenue that was a personal favorite hangout of mine on Saturdays.

I attended Sterling High School and felt privileged to have done so. The environment was encouraging and engaging. We knew our teachers and they were interested in our education and well-being. They didn't settle for mediocrity. Most of the materials we used were not up to par. We had second-hand books but that didn't stop us from receiving a quality education. We were well disciplined.

Sterling was more than a school. It was a close-knit community with a prestigious reputation for churning out competitive students. We took pride in being members of that community.

Some of the alumni include Greenville County Councilwoman Xanthene Norris (class of '46); state representative Ralph Anderson (class of '45); Dr. Thomas E. Kerns, the first African-American superintendent for the Greenville County School District (class of '49); Former Greenville County Councilwoman Lottie Gibson (class of '47); and Civil Rights Activist Jesse

Jackson (class of '59). I'm a graduate from the class of 1962 which comprised 114 students.

Sterling was the first black high school in Greenville and for a long time, it was the only black high school in Greenville. The other black high schools in Greenville County were Bryson, Washington, Beck and Lincoln.

When the desegregation of schools took place during the 1970's, many black students across the country found their academic stature and high school memories diluted and belittled after being forced to transfer and integrate into traditionally white schools.

Sterling seniors from the class of 1970, however, were fortunate to finish that year and graduate from their school. They were also able to publish a yearbook and received a diploma with the name Sterling High School on it.

Founded by Rev. Dr. D.M. Minus, Sterling opened up as a private institution, Greenvillle Academy, in 1896. It closed in 1913 and then reopened as Enoree Public High School in 1915. In 1929, the Greenville County School District purchased the building and the four acres it was located on and changed the name back to Sterling High School which graduated its first class of seniors in 1930.

Unfortunately, the school was "mysteriously" burned to the ground September 15, 1967 except for the gymnasium which today operates as a community center. According to a report by the fire marshal, the culprit was faulty wiring.

On September 15, 1967, in the dawn of desegregation, Sterling High was mysteriously destroyed by fire. This image shows the school in ruins after the fire. (Courtesy of the Greenville Cultural Exchange Center.)

*Photo is courtesy of the Greenville Cultural Exchange Center*

*Here I am at prom with my handsome date and long-time friend, James Brooks.*

*I am grateful to be a proud graduate of Sterling High School which provided a quality and nurturing learning environment.*

*Renowned educator Mary McLeod Bethune with Mr. J.E. Beck and Greenville County Schools Superintendent W.F. Loggins at a special dedication for Sterling in 1950*

I have so many fond memories. I remember hanging out in the band room listening to my peers practice. I remember when revered educator Mary McLeod Bethune visited the school in 1950 for a special dedication after the building underwent renovations. I loved the pep rallies. For me, there was nothing like our school spirit. We learned the cheers, one of which I recall as the following:

"Two bits!"

"Four bits!"

"Six bits a dollar!"

"All for Sterling, Stand up and holler!"

And here was our Alma Mater:

*Sterling High School, Sterling High School*

*Sterling High School, Bless her name!*

*Whether in defeat or victory!*

*We are loyal just the same;*

*So we'll cheer for Sterling High School*

*And for her we'll fight for fame*

*And we'll sing her praises loud in every land*

*Sterling High School, Bless her name!*

Sterling High School was the place where I met my first boyfriend: Paul Cooley. We dated for two and a half years. He was chivalrous, carrying my books and escorting me to every class. We went to the school dances and had lunch together. When you saw Paul, you saw me. He played the trumpet, was well dressed and smart as a whip. By that time, I had long accepted my "handicap." Paul thought I was beautiful and who was I to argue? Like most good times, it came to an end. He went into the military, and I went off to college.

I was a student at Benedict College when I heard through the grapevine about the fire that destroyed my beloved high school. I came home the next day. When I visited the site, it was still simmering. There were a lot of folks standing around staring in disbelief. Memories raced through my mind as I surveyed the ashy remnants—memories of walking through the hall, band practice and pep rallies and socializing in the cafeteria.

I remember one particular math teacher: Harriett Williams. My sister, Louella, was in her class. Ms. Williams was known for keeping an immaculate classroom. She kept a bucket and sponge near her desk. You didn't stand up against the walls or write on them. If you dared such, the bucket and sponge were all yours. Her students respected her classroom. She was the first person who came to mind because she was so particular about keeping her classroom neat and clean.

It was on a Friday night when the tragedy took place. A program happening inside the gymnasium was interrupted when someone informed the radio announcer/host that the building was on fire. He calmly asked everybody to stop what they were doing, form a line and go outside. He didn't panic or scream, "Fire!" So he was instrumental in helping to get everyone out of the building safely.

Like many of my peers and others in the community, I was shocked and distraught. How can a school be burned almost entirely to the ground? No clues? No suspects? I just couldn't believe it. I was never content with the story ending there. I spoke to the fire marshal and obtained a report out of Columbia. The report blamed faulty wiring. However, a news article I read said the school was "mysteriously" burned to the ground. The gymnasium did not burn up although the rest of the school did.

Years later, the gym was converted into Sterling Community Center, which is currently under the auspices of Greenville County. The center remains an important part of the community offering programs and services for youth and families. There's a monument at the intersection of Calhoun and Jenkins streets. A historical marker also stands on the corner of Pendleton Avenue and Calhoun Street. Both serve as valuable reminder of what was once one of the most influential institutions for blacks in Greenville.

Bronze statues of student figures in Downtown Greenville provide a prominent and vivid reminder of Sterling's legacy as well as a distinct representation of the Civil Rights Movement during the 1960s. The statues are located at the corner of Washington and Main Streets in front of the former Woolworth building where Sterling students conducted sit-ins and protests.

*These bronze statues downtown provide a vivid reminder of the importance of Sterling's legacy to the Greenville Community.*
*\*Photos are courtesy of Margaret Rose Media, LLC.*

*A monument for Sterling High stands near what is now the Sterling Community Center. *Photo courtesy of Margaret Rose Media, LLC.*

I didn't set out to write a book about Sterling High School but that's exactly what happened when I was asked by former schoolmates to update the school's history for our first reunion for all Sterling graduates. That reunion took place in 1990.

It was an emotional and nostalgic time. Graduates and former students came from all over the country to fellowship with each other for that special event. It was just so good seeing everybody.

*A South Carolina Historical Marker stands on the corner of Calhoun and Pendleton Streets in Greenville honoring the legacy of Sterling High School. *Photo courtesy of Margaret Rose Media, LLC.*

I delved into my shopping bag full of Sterling memorabilia—
from newspaper articles and school programs to old photos and
yearbooks. In the 1944 yearbook, there was a two-page history
of Sterling. When I finished updating that history, I ended up
with almost 20 pages!

*Sterling students took pride in producing quality memories for our
yearbook, The Torch.*

That was too much to print for a reunion so I had to shorten it.
However, my peers emphatically declared that my efforts be
not in vain and they encouraged me to write a book. I knew
absolutely nothing about writing a book but through the grace
of God, I did just that. I completed it in 1990 but it wasn't
published until three years later due to lack of funds.

Five hundred copies were finally published by A-Press Publishing Company. Word got around and I sold out within six months. It was, like so many events in my life, another unexpected blessing.

## Chapter 4: Call for Higher Learning

Before I attended Benedict College, I studied at Barber Scotia College in Concord, NC for one semester. I temporarily dropped out because of limited funds and sought full-time employment.

I was hired by The Rev. H.O. Mims Sr., the principal of Sterling High School at the time, to look after his mother-n-law, Mrs. L.L. Sewell. Mrs. Sewell was a retired school supervisor and piano instructor who needed consistent care.

I cared for her Monday through Friday from 8 a.m. to 5 p.m., cooking meals and doing other chores. Mrs. Sewell was one of those people, who despite coming off as stern initially, became a key figure on my path to getting an education.

She was brown skinned with noble features. She always wanted her meat and vegetables prepared a certain way and had no qualms about letting me know what she liked and didn't liked.

One day, she asked me why I wasn't in school. I told her about my one-semester experience at Barber Scotia, how I became homesick and how I could no longer afford it anyway being that my parents already had three other siblings in college.

"You need to be in school," said Mrs. Sewell. "Look, if I help you get back into college, will you go?"

"I reckon I would," I said. "But who would take care of you?"

"Don't worry about me," Mrs. Sewell said in a caring but stern tone. "I will find someone else to take care of me."

Mrs. Sewell made it her personal mission to get me back into school. She met with my father and called Dr. J.A. Bacoats, president of Benedict College in Columbia. My father and I intently listened as she spoke to Dr. Bacoats over the phone.

"Will you provide funds to help Ruth Ann?" Mrs. Sewell asked Dr. Bacoats.

"Yes, I will," he said. "Tell her to be here in two weeks and come to my office."

And I did. I registered and had all of the books and supplies I needed for my journey of higher learning.

I entered Benedict with the highest math score for a test given to incoming first-year students. I give credit to my Sterling education for that. I would tutor my peers in math and was often asked by my professors why I didn't major in the subject.

*I enjoyed my years studying at Benedict College. Here I am doing homework in my dorm*

I really wanted to be a social worker, but Benedict College didn't have a major for that so I chose social studies as my main course of study. I graduated from Benedict without owing a single penny to the school. When I came home for Christmas break, I called Rev. Mims informing him that I had completed my courses.

*My graduation ceremony at Benedict College*

"Have you done your student teaching?" he asked.

"I have no desire to be a teacher," I said. Rev. Mims told me to return to Benedict, take some elected courses and do student teaching. After completing my electives, I did my student teaching at Lincoln High School in Taylors where I met Mr. William Flemming.

He was one of the best social studies teachers in Greenville County Schools. I was so impressed and inspired by him, I had a change of heart and pursued teaching as a career.

Before I landed my first teaching job at Bryson High School, I had another goal: getting my driver's license. My father agreed to help me get a car if I got my license and a steady job.

I taught at Bryson for a year in subjects other than social studies. Mr. A. Maceo Anderson was my mentor. He was one of the best principals ever. He supported and respected his teachers. He even sponsored a Christmas party one year out of gratitude for his staff.

Mr. Anderson was a fair man, dignified and approachable. He walked the halls and didn't have to say much to receive respect from teachers and students. He wasn't mean but he was stern. He was no push-over.

He let you know what he liked and what he didn't like. One day, I came to work late because I was stopped by a police officer for speeding. When I entered the school, I saw Mr. Anderson waiting for me at the front door and I showed him my speeding ticket. His response? "I guess you'll wake up sooner." I wasn't late anymore after that. Mr. Anderson expected a lot but he also gave a lot.

There were no social studies teaching positions available in Greenville County so after a year, I began searching for work elsewhere. I got a job teaching at Coffee Junior High in Douglas, Ga. and became roommates with a colleague, Evelyn Fussell.

While working at Coffee, I met and became close friends with Eugene, a physical education teacher. He was a tall, handsome, dark-skinned football player with bowed legs.

It was the 1969-1970 school year. The student body at Coffee was already integrated but the number of black faculty there was rather sparse. So Eugene and I hung out together. We were attracted to each other and relished in each other's company going to clubs, movies and restaurants. That time led to more time. I eventually fell in love, and I later got pregnant.

His reaction to my pregnancy was hurtful but I accepted it. I had to. He did not step up to the plate as I hoped he would. There was no marriage proposal. No wedding. No fairy tale ending. Still, I was not about to get rid of my baby.

Reality set in quick and hard. At first, I had absolutely no clue as to what I was going to do. Here I am, the educated daughter of a minister, a product of a well-groomed family---pregnant and not married!!! What would my parents and siblings think?! It was almost too much to bear at the time.

Back then, if you were a female teacher, pregnant and not married, your career was in jeopardy at best. So for several weeks, I kept the fact that I was going to be a mother to myself. I felt so alone, rejected and ashamed. I suppose the good news was I didn't start showing until late in my pregnancy. So no one suspected anything.

I called my brother Willie Charles and told him about my situation. He called my sister Maybelle and then she called everybody else. I went ahead and took several deep breaths after that, but not before I cried my share of tears prior to letting the cat out of the bag.

My parents, of course, were shocked, hurt and disappointed. I didn't want to go back home so at the invitation of my brother Grady I moved to Atlanta. He told me about a shelter for pregnant single women.

I moved in June and my son, Benjamin Brown, was born August 2, 1970. I didn't name him but I did get to hold him for a few minutes. The doctor assured me that my son would be OK.

After he was born, my social worker brought Benjamin back to Greenville where I went to family court and I gave up my rights as the biological mother. I felt like I would have had a tough time getting a job as a single mother. I wanted him to be adopted by a loving couple who would be better capable of taking care of him financially.

Aside from telling my parents and siblings, I never shared the fact that I had a child with anyone else. I remember sitting in church every Mother's Day feeling a bit empty. When all the mothers were asked to stand, I remained seated.

Two months after Benjamin was born, his father called inquiring about his son's whereabouts. By that time, I had already given him up for adoption. I told him, "I don't know." That was the end of that conversation and we never spoke again after that. Years later, I was reunited with our son. (I will share more about this later in the book).

Prior to the lovely reunion with my son in 2012, God placed yet another blessing in my life. He came in the form of a black, white and beige puppy. I named him Benji. I never thought of myself as a dog person but I quickly grew to love this dog in all of his persistence and loyalty.

There's a time and season for everything. The time when Benji and I found each other was around the same time, my son, Benjamin, decided to look for me, his birth mother. This was in 2011. A close friend told me, "Benji was sent to watch over you until your son found you." Yep. God planned it that way. I believe it with all my heart.

I find it interesting that I unwittingly named something I loved with a name similar to the one given to my son. I also found it interesting that Benji died the day after I was reunited with my son.

## Chapter 5: Unexpected Guest

I met Benji one warm summer day in 2011. I pulled up in my driveway and was unexpectedly welcomed by a puppy. He greeted me as I opened my car door.

At first, I tried to shoo him away. I walked past him into the house. He followed me to the back door, with a heart-tugging stare and wagging his tail ever so playfully. The next morning I opened my back door and there he was again. His stare followed me to my car and he watched intently as I drove away.

When I came home, he was there again waiting for me like a loyal companion. This went on for about three months. I never fed or petted him during this time to avoid an emotional attachment. Despite my so-called tough love, a bond eventually formed.

I began feeding him but I didn't let him inside. His welcoming became more exuberant as he began making attempts to hop in my lap as I would get in or out of the car. Every morning and afternoon, he faithfully walked me to and from my car.

One day, it rained very hard accompanied by thundering and lightning. Hours later, I found him soaked at my back door and allowed him inside the house. I folded a blanket on the floor in my hallway.

Apparently, he found it cozy and comfy. He went straight to that spot and curled up. He was such a good house dog. And he never answered to anyone but me.

It was as though God put that adorable little creature in my life—this small but unexpected blessing—as a simple reminder of how much HE loves me, while revealing to me my own nurturing instincts.

Despite how much I enjoyed caring for him, rental policy took precedent over compassion. I was not allowed to have pets. Eventually I had to give him away so I blessed a colleague of mine who was looking for a good house dog. Although I wanted to keep Benji, I knew he and my colleague would enjoy each other's company. And they did, hitting it off right away.

I still visited Benji occasionally and he never ceased to show me that love and excitement he displayed from the first day we met. So when I heard that one day Benji had passed, I felt a deep sadness and void.

I don't always know why things happen the way they do but I take comfort in knowing that God does. So I can no longer think my tears are in vain. Over the years, as I've grown stronger in my faith, I tend to pray about everything. I'm often reminded of the following scriptures:

***Ecclesiastes 3: 1-8*** *"To everything, there is a season, A time for every purpose under heaven....A time to weep, and a time to laugh; a time to mourn, and a time to dance...a time to tear, and a time to sow.... A time to keep silence, a time to speak, a time to love...."*

***Romans 8:28*** *says, "And we know that God causes all things to work together for the good of those who love God, to those who are called according to His purpose."*

## Chapter 6: It runs in the family

I was thrilled when someone donated a hard copy of the best-selling book, *Roots* by Alex Haley to the Greenville Cultural Exchange Center. I actually saw the movie before I read the book so it made the reading that much more intriguing.

I also attended a book signing at Furman University where several people waited in line to get Haley's autograph and a few minutes to chat with him. It was pretty exciting. When it was my turn to get his autograph, I told him about my vision and plans for an African-American history museum. He was cordial and said that was very nice. I was completely fascinated with the fact that Haley was able to trace his roots all the way back to Africa.

*Meeting best-selling author Alex Haley was one of my career highlights.*

I think everybody is entitled to know the connections to their families. And when you find out your family history, it will change your life.

In 1971, I was hired at Northwood Middle School as a seventh grade social studies teacher. While at Northwood, I initiated an elective course in genealogy in 1979. It was spirit week and teachers had the opportunity to teach something other than their usual academic subject. One teacher offered basket weaving lessons. Another provided a class on quilt making. I decided to do genealogy.

I was interested in this and excited about it but I had no idea what I was doing. I quickly learned. I took a crash course at the local library on how to teach genealogy to seventh graders.

The course at Northwood was supposed to run for three weeks but it turned into a year-long course. Students became very enthusiastic about tracing their family history. As my students would present their family history before class, it dawned on me halfway through the semester, I knew nothing about my own family history.

So I announced to my family during Thanksgiving dinner that I would launch an official research of our family history. I would spend every Saturday researching my family history. In one year, I had researched my entire family history all the way back to Africa. I brought up the idea of planning a family reunion with hopes of someone else taking up that mantle. Instead, I got "stuck" with holding it.

So I said to myself that if I can find a decent, inexpensive venue where my family can congregate, I would plan our reunion. I also surveyed relatives in passing when I was out and about, whether it was in grocery stores, restaurants or at the post office. I asked them, "If I plan a family reunion, would you come?" They all answered, "Yes."

I had no idea how it would turn out. All I knew was that I wanted to be a part of this special family celebration. With the grace of God, things fell into place. I started the reunion committee comprised of different branches of my family: cousins, nephews, nieces, etc.

Our first family reunion took place in 1982 at Rock Hill No. 1 Baptist Church. My daddy was baptized there. There's also a gravesite located on the grounds where a lot of my descendants are buried. So the location held special significance.

*Picture of 1982 Butler Family Reunion at Rock Hill #1 Baptist Church*

My family tree boasts several ministers and restaurant owners. Those with food expertise helped create a menu and each family brought a dish. It was all free.

Committee members collected addresses and phone numbers and mailed letters. We published a directory and a booklet that traced our family history all the way back to Africa.

There was such camaraderie involved and as things progressed, that spirit of teamwork increased. People started jumping on a very special bandwagon.

We ended up having 300 people over a three-day period. Relatives from all over the country came. About 19 states were represented. We even organized a Butler choir.

They started coming in on a Friday. Saturday we had a program with the Rev. C.C. Stewart Sr. as our guest speaker. He was excellent. The title of his speech was "It Runs in the Family." He spoke about how different accomplishments, talents and skills are passed on from generation to generation.

*Reunions are a treasured tradition for my family.*

My nephew, Steve Butler, for instance, was a good Little League baseball pitcher.

I explained to him while researching our family, I discovered two of my brothers were very good pitchers and that my daddy bragged about being a good pitcher. As I mentioned earlier, my dad had his own pitch called "The Dusty Mule."

So I told my nephew, "It just runs in the family."

"Aunt Ruth, what are you talking about?" he asked.

That's when I told him about his two uncles and grandfather.

Once you find out how names and talents are passed down, it gives you an instant sense of pride. A lot of people are doing things and don't realize how or why they are capable of doing such. That's because it runs in the family.

I strongly feel that everybody is entitled to know their connections whether that person is adopted or a biological offspring. When you find out your family history, it will change your life. You can thoughtfully reflect on your inheritance— an inheritance that has more value than any dollar, stock or bond.

Your perspective about everything is elevated -- from geographical destinations and professional lineage to personality traits and family medical history.

Researching my family tree further fueled my curiosity. I became known as the lady in the library. Every Saturday, I would come in the library around the same time as the security guard and left around the same time he did. I was there from open to close trying to soak up as much knowledge and history as I could. I brought snacks so I could stay all day long.

One day I was researching my family history on microfiche. Scanning the 1870 census for Edgefield, SC, I discovered Easter and Simon Butler, slaves who were freed in 1865. "I found my family!" I shouted. I was so excited. The entire library heard that excitement.

*Once upon a time, The Greenville County Library was located on McBee Ave. It was one of my favorite hangouts on Saturdays.*

## Chapter 7: Staying Power

I knew the good Lord was planning something special when He gave me the vision to start the Greenville Cultural Exchange Center.

In hindsight, I knew this was the purpose God set for me. When God has a specific plan set in motion for you, no one or nothing else can thwart it. You have to stay the course and remain faithful. While we tend to get discouraged and stray away from Him, God is always there even when we think He's not.

I know He has always been there for me during the ups, downs and near-misses in my life. I reflect with fascination on a number of near-death experiences. With each experience, I said to myself, 'God has kept me here for a reason.' Sometimes God will have us go through situations so we can see how awesome He really is.

I remember how God kept me after a serious health crisis. My gallbladder burst and I had to be rushed to the hospital. One morning I went to the bank and an employee mentioned how I "was glowing." I replied "thank you," thinking the glow was complimentary. Little did I know my skin's brightness stemmed from a health situation that would quickly spiral into a life-threatening crisis.

I called my friend Helen Pinson while I was at work. (I was working as a secretary for a church part time in the mornings while managing the Greenville Cultural Exchange Center in the afternoons.)

I told Helen about the "compliments" I received.

"Are you yellow?" she asked.

I looked in the mirror. "Yeah."

Suspecting I had jaundice, she quipped, "Get your tail to a doctor!"

"Babies have that," I said, brushing off her concern.

She got very demanding, calling me by first and middle name.

I went to the doctor later that day but not before I met with another close friend, Mary Dixon.

I caught up with Mary at Pete's Restaurant on Pendleton Street and told her about my dilemma. This was a Friday and I was planning a festival for local artists Saturday—the very next day.

I was thinking to myself I don't have time to see a doctor. I don't have time to be sick. My focus was on making the art festival at the center a huge success.

That didn't matter because Mary also had a sense of urgency about this.

She said, "You are yellow! You need to go and see a doctor!" Mary was just as adamant as Helen about me seeing a doctor

ASAP. I did as my dear friends demanded but first, I went back to the center and ate my lunch.

Fortunately, for me, Mary worked at a local clinic so I asked her if she could get a doctor to see me as soon as possible. I was thinking it's probably just a virus and if I can get some pills or a shot, I should be back to normal in no time.

Mary promised to have a doctor waiting to see me when I arrived at the clinic. When I arrived, two physicians were waiting to examine me. I gave one of them a hyped spill about this awesome museum I started: "Ma'am have you ever heard of the Greenville Cultural Exchange Center? I have to plan for this festival tomorrow. I have all of these artists coming."

I rambled on completely clueless as to what was happening.

I waited for their diagnosis. Both doctors, along with Mary, returned to the examination room and informed me that they contacted the emergency room at Greenville Memorial Hospital and staff were waiting for me.

"They're waiting for me?" I was perplexed. "I don't have time," I said. "I'll go Monday. I really appreciate everything you've done."

Mary wasn't having it. "You're going to get your tail to the hospital!" she said. "Are you driving?"

"Yeah, I'm driving."

She even threatened to dial 911. I told her I would go.

"Well, can I at least go back to the center first?" I asked. "NO!" Mary snapped. "Get your tail to the emergency room! They're waiting for you right now!"

"Are you Ms. Butler?" The man inquired at the emergency's entrance.

"Yes," I said most cautiously.

"This wheelchair is for you," he replied.

About five doctors at the hospital examined me. It didn't matter that such a cloud of wonder hung over me. I couldn't stop running my mouth, going on and on about the Greenville Cultural Exchange Center trying to converse with staff about the center and my plans for the festival.

Apparently, God had other plans for me. Results from a full-body X-ray sent doctors into a frenzy. *What was all the excitement about?* I asked myself. They were hustling, organizing and preparing—like a bunch of firefighters responding to a fire alarm.

I was told they were getting ready to operate on me.

"No sir," I said, still unaware of how serious my condition was. I was too wrapped up in my thoughts about the center and the upcoming arts festival. "You're going to have to operate on Monday."

They were oblivious to my anxious chatter. I was impatient and all I could think about was: *The center needs me. There was so much to do prior to the festival. I didn't have time for this!*

Or so I thought.

The doctors informed me that I had been walking around with a burst gallbladder for about two weeks! My whole body was shutting down by the second. One of the physicians told me that I was the sickest person in the entire hospital and that I would not make it to Monday.

I couldn't believe it. I felt OK. I wasn't in any pain and the doctors couldn't understand why I wasn't in any pain. The doctors said under "normal circumstances," someone in my condition should have been in a lot of pain. But I suppose this wasn't a normal situation, not with God being a part of it anyway.

Prior to this, I was relatively healthy and had not been sick for 20 years. I don't even recall popping an aspirin for a headache.

During surgery, doctors had to remove all of the gallbladder stones that ruptured throughout my body. I woke up after the surgery hooked up to so many devices. I stayed in the hospital for eight days. Doctors informed me that I should not work or drive for five weeks. I was supposed to relax, but I've been told I can be stubborn so those instructions proved rather difficult to follow. Nevertheless, I did what was necessary. I stayed away from the center for five weeks. During that time, I had to resist the urge to just get up and go simply because I felt good at the moment.

My brother, Grady, took care of things at the center the day of the festival. The news media and others from the community were present. My absence was obvious but the festival took place as scheduled and the center kept running despite my medical emergency.

That's one of those close calls that I'll never forget. I'm grateful to the doctors and medical staff who took care of me but I also credit my dear friends, Helen Pinson and Mary Dixon for saving my life. If it weren't for them, I wouldn't have been at the hospital in the first place.

The Lord took care of me, the center, the festival and the staff who operated on me. I'm grateful for His mercy and sovereignty. It's good to be able to sit back as if in a recliner or rocking chair and marvel at how God has protected me and what He has brought me through.

Helen was also the one who pushed me into applying for disability later on when the Greenville Cultural Exchange Center was temporarily shut down. I remember telling her, "Helen, I got to get out here and find me another job."

"Well, you need to go on and file for disability," she said.

"I'm not disabled," I said a bit haughtily.

She quipped in her sassy but loving way, "Silly! You were born disabled!"

"Oh," I said.

*****

I had a couple of other close calls. I was in two car accidents. Both incidents involved my vehicles going airborne and being totaled. I walked away practically unscathed.

I was working for Neighborhoods in Action as a transportation/housing coordinator at the time of the first accident. I was on my way to check on the Greenville Cultural Exchange Center when a man rammed into my car on the driver's side. It happened at the intersection of Memminger Street and Arlington Avenue.

I had the right of way. Apparently, the other driver wasn't paying attention to that. When he ran into my car, it instantly went airborne. The impact knocked my car over to the opposite side of the street near a fire hydrant. The windows cracked and the entire bottom of my car dropped out.

The only door that would open was on the driver's side. I walked away minus serious injury. The next year, I was involved in another accident that resulted in another miracle. I visited a friend in Simpsonville and was headed back to Greenville. It was not too long after sunset.

The accident took place near the intersection of Harrison Bridge Road and Main Street.

I did not see any construction cones around the area I was about to pass. Suddenly, I felt an incredible thud and sinking feeling. I accidentally drove into a very large and deep hole dug for railroad tracks—wide and deep enough for a car to stay in there and not be found.

But my car didn't stay in there. It fell inside the hole and immediately came out as though it bounced right out of there. Again, the windows cracked and the bottom of my car dropped out. I opened the door on the driver's side, got out, flagged down a driver and asked him to call the police.

My friend Linda Murray whom I'd just visited came to pick me up.

The officer inspected the hole and said, "Ma'am, did you go down in there?"

"Yes. I did."

"Ma'am, did you know you could have been stuck down there and no one would have known you were down there?!"

Pause.

His countenance smeared with shock and disbelief looking at the hole again.

"And you went down there?" he asked again.

"Yes," I said.

I was still a little shaken so I didn't want to think about what could have been. I was just glad I was out of there and able to walk away.

Later on I called another friend of mine, John Daniel Mosley, to assist me with getting another car. Mosley was a car salesman.

"You just don't wreck a car, Ruth. You total it!" he said.

These days, I drive a white Nissan Sentra, which you'll often find parked safely at the Greenville Cultural Exchange Center.

## Chapter 8: History in the Making

T he Greenville Cultural Exchange Center was a mustard seed that God watered, planted and helped flourish during good times and bad.

In 1985 I, along with a group of friends and colleagues traveled to Knoxville, TN to visit the Beck Cultural Exchange Center. I was working as a social studies teacher for the Greenville County School District at the time and saw an obvious need for preservation of African-American history in Upstate South Carolina.

I taught European history at Northwood Middle School and there in the hallways, every February I displayed cases filled with black history artifacts. I became known as the lady who had the black history information.

I was also on the committee that reviewed textbooks at Northwood and noticed that material and resources on black history were rather limited.

I've always been interested in African-American history and collected black history artifacts, Ebony magazines, programs, obits, black newspapers, etc. and collected and stored in my attic. I used them for case displays at schools.

I found out about an African-American history museum in Knoxville via my sister, Nina Butler-Lewis, a high school teacher who lived and worked in Knoxville. So I made it a goal that I would check it out next time I visited the city: The Beck Cultural Exchange Center.

Once I toured the center, I became even more inspired and motivated to open something similar for Greenville. I was impressed with their three-fold purpose: providing archival resources for students, serving as a meeting place for organizations and providing individual and group tours.

I felt like Greenville needed such a facility, but at the time I was too busy with work, church and Girl Scouts. (I used to have one of the largest troops in Greenville.) Besides, I wasn't sure if I would be able to even pull it off because I had visited only a few museums and I knew nothing about starting one.

My sister, Nina, kept encouraging me and I began to solicit input from various people to see if this project was feasible.

Everyone that I spoke to embraced the idea. So I began searching for a site.

Colleagues and I would frequently meet to analyze how such an enterprise could become a reality in Greenville. We organized a steering committee and met at different places: my house, Phillis Wheatley Center and the Austin Music Academy, a private music school. The school was housed inside a two-story home on the corner of Arlington Avenue and Sumner Street.

I really liked the layout and interior of the academy and spoke with the director, John Hunter, a Sterling alumni, about leasing space. The home's design was similar to the Beck Cultural Exchange Center.

Hunter initially declined my offer to lease space in the house. However, a few months later, Hunter's neighbor died and he got an offer to buy his neighbor's house. So he came back to me making an offer asking me which house would I like to buy. I chose the one on the corner of Arlington and Sumner where Hunter housed his music academy.

Located at 700 Arlington Avenue in the West End community, the historic craftsman-style manor home became the place where archives of history came alive, where the public traveled back in time via tours and talks. The Greenville Cultural Exchange Center officially opened August 22, 1987 with a public ribbon-cutting ceremony.

Former state senator Theo Mitchell cut the ribbon. It was an awesome feeling of accomplishment. Still, I had no idea of what I was getting myself into. At that time, I did not see the financial turbulence ahead, the city of Greenville closing the center, folks who would smile in my face but work towards getting the center closed, and the folks who wanted to (and still) want to ransack my personal artifacts for their personal benefit.

Establishing a museum in Greenville that's dedicated to African-American history has always been a personal passion of mine. While The Greenville Cultural Exchange Center is my brainchild, my purpose is larger than my personal passion.

Sometimes when black history is incorporated into a mainstream display, people get highlights, tidbits and soundbites instead of meaningful details and specific incidents. I believe black museums are a special treasure here in the United States. Unfortunately, they are also a struggling breed.

I was featured in a *Greenville News* article by veteran journalist Ron Barnett titled "Cultural Exchange faces common struggle." (January 25, 2015). Here's an excerpt:

"Black history gets its share of attention each February, but the places where people can go year-round to come face-to-face with the excruciating truth about slavery and to encounter the milestones of the Civil Rights movement often find it difficult to survive."

It turns out black museums across the country are struggling to overcome financial difficulties --from The Underground Railroad Freedom Center in Cincinnati to The International Civil Rights Museum in Greensboro, NC, according to the article.

This certainly comes as no shocker to me. The struggle to expose *all* aspects of our history is very real.

\*\*\*\*\*

I called my business plan for the center a survival plan. You've got to have people behind you who have a passion for what you are trying to do and accomplish. I am not ashamed to ask for help when it comes to a worthy cause. I'm not afraid to work hard at keeping the center afloat and I'm not afraid to give back knowing that the Lord will provide because it's not always about money. For more than 29 years, the center has survived on the generosity of many folks in Greenville and I'm forever grateful.

My goal is to increase awareness and appreciation of the contributions made by black people here in the Upstate and to promote economic empowerment in the black community. Much of our history has been ignored for so many years. Still, there is so much that is not talked about or discussed.

For instance, many people know about Dr. Martin Luther King Jr. and the Civil Rights Movement, but how many know about the horrific incidents involving public lynchings in South Carolina or the Jim Crow laws that terrorized and wreaked havoc in black communities across the South?

While the Civil Rights Movement is a very important aspect of American history, it is not the only segment of black history. There's more that needs to be highlighted, such as the economic impact of slavery, reconstruction, Jim Crow laws and the lynching of Willie Earle (the last noted public lynching in South Carolina).

I also wonder how many people are aware of the notable achievements of blacks who lived in Greenville, such as Wilfred Walker, the first African-American radio announcer and sports broadcaster in South Carolina and the late Tuskegee pilot, Paul Adams. (My father officiated the marriage of Adams and his wife, Alda.)

I did not start the Greenville Cultural Exchange Center to simply have my own. I wanted to share my vision to help the public better understand the importance of accurate research and to see how we are all connected when it comes to history, no matter our ethnic or socio-economic background.

Nobody gave me any kind of guidelines. I lacked business expertise. I did research and some planning but a lot of it was trial and error. That was OK because with every challenge I overcame, I took away a valuable lesson and moved a step closer to God.

As I stumbled along, I discovered I needed several things, such as an occupancy permit, a permit for the business sign and a dozen parking spaces for which I had to uproot a tree in the middle of the backyard. I went to Greenville City Hall to do a presentation about what I had seen in Knoxville, TN and about what I could do for Greenville. Bill Workman was the mayor at the time. I didn't even know I had to sign up to speak.

Prior to the meeting's conclusion, Workman asked if anyone else wanted to speak before council. I emphatically raised my hand.

"Who are you?" he asked.

"Ruth Ann Butler," I said.

He told me I had three minutes to make my presentation. I took 45.

I had everybody spellbound because nobody had heard of such. Workman said he would support me. The City of Greenville donated $10,000 prior to the center's opening.

Workman wrote a letter to Greenville County requesting that the county match those funds. The request was approved and those matching funds went toward a first-year operational budget and renovation costs.

Over the years, the center has served as an educational and research resource for students of all ages, provided historic preservation assistance to churches, families and various organizations as well as hosted numerous tours, genealogy workshops, exhibits, youth functions and holiday events.

*It was always a pleasure when the amazing Peg Leg Bates paid a visit.*

Fountain Inn native and dancing extraordinaire Peg Leg Bates would come and see me every time he visited Greenville. Civil Rights Activist Jesse Jackson visited the center several times. We also held receptions for internationally recognized artist Jonathan Green and renowned genealogist, author and lecturer Tony Burroughs.

*Greenville native and Civil Rights Activist Jesse Jackson was one of our many distinguished visitors at the center.*

*I also had the privilege of meeting the renowned genealogist Tony Burroughs.*

## Timeline of the Greenville Cultural Exchange Center

**January 27, 1986-** Greenville Cultural Exchange Center acquires tax-exempt status under Section 501(c)(3) of the IRS Code.

**May 27, 1987-** the American Federal Bank of Greenville loans the center $65,000. to purchase an old Victorian building to house center.

**August 22, 1987-** Greenville Cultural Exchange Center officially opens its doors with ribbon-cutting ceremony.

**August 22, 1997-** Greenville Cultural Exchange Center celebrates 10-year anniversary

**May 25, 2001-** City of Greenville closes the doors of the Greenville Cultural Exchange Center due to structural damage.

**March 2002-** The "Friends of the Center" campaign headed by Helen Pinson and WJMZ/107.3 radio station raises $70,000 enabling renovations and re-occupancy.

**April 26, 2003-** Greenville Cultural Exchange Center reopens.

**April 4, 2005 –** Greenville Cultural Exchange Center hosts its first Women Making History Awards banquet

**August 22, 2012**- Greenville Cultural Exchange Center celebrates 25-year anniversary

**August 22, 2017**- Greenville Cultural Exchange Center's upcoming 30-year anniversary

*Ruth Ann with former Greenville Mayor Bill Workman and John
Hunter, a Sterling Alumni and director of the Austin Music
Academy*

*The city's closing of the Greenville Cultural Exchange Center in 2001 was an unexpected setback but it did not deter me from doing what I needed to do to reopen.*

## Chapter 9: Troubled Times Ahead

1967- Sterling High School was burned.

*The Greenville Cultural Exchange Center has been the target of vandalism and threats over the years. This bulldog statue was thrown through one of my windows downstairs. I took it and put it inside one of my display cases as a reminder of God's protection and my fight to keep the center alive and thriving. *Photo courtesy of Margaret Rose Media, LLC.*

I refuse to live in fear.

And when you do what you're supposed to do, God will take care of you. That does not mean you live trouble free. It means God hears your prayers and sees what you're up against. However, with obedience and perseverance come many blessings.

There was a period when I maintained my teaching career while still serving as the executive director for the Greenville Cultural Exchange Center.

I prayed about it and decided to take a leave of absence from teaching thinking that it would only be a two-year hiatus. My hope was to hand over the mantle during that time and return to teaching, but life as we often know, doesn't always go according to our plans. I didn't find anybody willing to step up and commit to helping me manage the center and I never returned to teaching full-time.

My heart was always at the Greenville Cultural Exchange Center. I worked various jobs while operating the center including working as a church secretary and a transportation/housing coordinator. I also took on a part-time teaching position for an after-school program. These jobs allowed me the flexibility to work at the center.

I never would have known I was a researcher if I had remained in the classroom. I only found my passion for researching after I resigned from teaching full-time.

However, there was a price to be paid for following my passion and dreams.

Over the years, The Greenville Cultural Exchange Center has received a number of threats and was vandalized. One time, someone threw a bulldog statue into my front window. I now have the statue on display in honor of the South Carolina State University mascot, which happens to be a bulldog. It also serves as a reminder of God's protection and my fight to keep the center alive and thriving.

On May 17, 2001, I was fired as a church secretary. Then eight days later, the city condemned and closed the center.

I was distraught and discouraged but not defeated.

God's grace proved sufficient once more. In my distress and at the strong urging of a friend, I filed for disability. I never did before then. In less than four months, I was approved for receiving benefits.

Relationship-building is very important. I will drop and stop for certain people that I know have my back. You can't treat people any kind of way. You can have all the good looks, money, talent, skills and education in the world but none of that means anything if you don't know how to treat people.

When the center shut down, people brought me groceries and a local auto mechanic volunteered to fix my car. As shocked and distraught as I was about the center's closing, I was more grateful for those who came to my rescue.

I worked diligently to comply with whatever the city requested and the center eventually reopened. Things were starting to turn around for the better.

## Chapter 10: A very special reunion

God has kept me through all my difficulties and I knew He was keeping me for something else very special.

Things really came full circle when I was reunited with my son, Benjamin Brown.

He was born in Atlanta August 2, 1970. He was brought back to Greenville and placed in foster care. He was later adopted at three years old by Ordie and Corine Brown of St. George, SC where he was raised.

Benjamin said he is grateful for his adoptive family and loves them very much. He grew up on a farm in St. George and overall, had a happy childhood.

Benjamin knew he was adopted since he was six years old. However, what he didn't know was that he was adopted at three years old. He thought he was adopted when he was an infant. He didn't know he was in foster care for three years prior to being adopted.

He found this out after inquiring about his baby pictures.

"My parents didn't have any," he said. "So I was curious about the lack of baby photos. I had two pictures of me as a child: one of me in a walker and the other was taken when I was about three years old wearing a red jumpsuit in somebody's backyard."

And for a while, it never bothered him that much. "I just went through life and never asked too many questions," Benjamin said. But his curiosity lingered. Benjamin kept noticing something was missing as he scanned through the family albums: pictures of his parents holding him when he was a baby.

Benjamin said he also noticed two dates on his birth certificate: August 2 and August 20. For 42 years, Benjamin said he assumed that his adoptive parents came to Atlanta and picked him up and took him back to South Carolina around Aug. 20— while he was an infant.

"So I went to my sister and asked her, 'where are all my baby pictures and pictures of mom and dad holding me as a child?'"

"What do you mean?" said his sister, Ordrine Brown Jordan, who is seven years older than Benjamin. "We didn't get you until you were three years old."

I said, "What?"

They went back and forth in a verbal tennis match.

She finally said, "Listen! I was there when we got you! Go ask dad."

Still perplexed and longing for answers, Benjamin did just that. His father had him fetch a file located in an old family footlocker. This file included a picture of him as a foster child.

Benjamin was already on a slow and evolving path of wanting to find me, his biological mother, two years prior but didn't push his quest until he felt it was time. Discovering that he was adopted at 3 years old motivated him more. It was more than a year after his adoptive mom passed when Benjamin decided to pursue his biological roots.

"Everybody wants to know where they came from," he said. "I wanted to find out what happened."

Like mother, like son.

*****

It was November 28, 2012 when I received a voice mail message that would change the rest of my life. It was from a woman named Rachel calling from an agency in Atlanta that helps adoptees and biological parents find each other. After listening to the message, I immediately felt it pertained to my son.

"This call is for Ruth Ann Butler," said the voice on the answering machine. "I'm calling from Atlanta. It's about a private matter. If you are Ruth Ann Butler, please give me a call back."

I called back the next morning.

"Good morning. I'm Ruth Ann Butler returning your call."

"I need to ask you a question," the woman on the other end said. There was a brief pause—deep, suspenseful silence.

"Did you ever live in Atlanta?" she asked.

"Yes," I replied calmly. My heart raced during our conversation. "I was in Atlanta August 2, 1970."

"Well, I think you know why I'm calling," she said.

"Yes," I said. "Is this pertaining to my son?"

She confirmed such. My son hired her to find me via Adoption Reunion.com.

The woman from the agency said searches are usually not that quick. I didn't get married so it helped that my last name was the same. With the exception of Benedict College and the nine months I stayed in Georgia, I remained in Greenville all of my life.

I always said to myself that I was going to keep my information open in case my son decided to look for me.

"I told him it would take about three to five months to find you," Rachel said. Apparently, it took a lot less time than that. In less than two weeks, they were onto me. She had access to all the birth certificates in Georgia and found my name, which she Googled. After they compared our photos, they were pretty certain.

My son was shocked. They contacted him before they contacted me. He had already planned his Christmas vacation thinking that it would be awhile before I was found. But his plans quickly changed.

However, before my son and I could talk on the phone, the agency sent me a 16-page document in the mail. I was informed of all my rights. I needed to sign the paperwork before any communication could take place between me and my son.

I didn't think they were going to send a picture and I had never seen a picture of Benjamin. I was standing in the middle of my living room thumbing through the documents when I came across a picture of my son. I just stood there in awe and forgot about the documents. I had to show my siblings.

I called my brother, Grady. "Grady! Grady! He looks just like me!" Grady said, "Yeah, yeah." I went to his house and showed him the picture. He was casually sitting in front of the television watching football. When I showed him the picture, he forgot about TV, abruptly sat up and snatched the photo out of my hand. "We don't need to have a meeting." (I was going to have a meeting with my siblings to decide what I should do.)

Like myself, Grady knew Benjamin was blood family from the moment he laid eyes on Benjamin's photo. No questions asked. No meetings were needed to discuss whether or not this man was my son. There was nothing to be uncertain about. He and I both knew what I needed to do. I had all the necessary documents notarized by Judge Robert Jenkins and mailed them back as soon as possible.

I called my sister, Louella who was grocery shopping at the time. I told her that someone from an agency called me about my son. There was a pause. "Louella?" I said. I could only imagine her reaction and facial expression.

"I'm still standing," she said.

My other sister, Maybelle, was a bit more vocal. I called her while she was getting her car repaired. She yelled out in excitement after hearing the news about my son. People around her asked if she was OK. I said, "Maybelle, close your mouth!"

As I look back on these moments, I can't help but chuckle about how God allowed things to unfold the way he did.

*Mother and son quality time at the beach.*

When my son and I first spoke over the phone, I was thrilled and humbled to hear his voice. We talked for at least two hours. After looking me up on the Internet, he said, "I see you've been busy. I've got a famous mama!"

*Benjamin with his wife, Alison and their children, Aiden, 2 and Mia, 4*

The lady from the agency suggested that our first face-to-face encounter be in private. So it would be just the two of us. I was excited and extremely nervous at the same time.

I was in such a fog over my son's visit, I couldn't even decorate for the holidays. I usually take pride in decorating the center because my birthday is on Christmas. But when I got that call from Rachel, all I could do was remove the decorations from the attic. I brought them from the attic and set them on a long table downstairs. They sat in boxes for about a week.

*Family Reunion: Here I am with my son Benjamin and my precious granddaughter, Mia*

Thankfully, a dear friend, Michelle Simmons, came over and noticed I was in no mood for decorating so she offered to do it for me. The fireplace was adorned with wreaths. Poinsettias added a fresh look to tables throughout and a tall Christmas tree lit up an exhibit room near the kitchen. The atmosphere was a little brighter. Michelle's efforts encouraged my holiday spirit. And I was ready to receive the best Christmas gift ever.

My son and I met each other for the first time December 21, 2012, more than four decades after the heart-wrenching experience of giving him up for adoption. It was a moment neither of us will forget. Our private meeting took place on a sunny, crisp and cold afternoon.

We were both nervous, excited and anxious. The doorbell rang. I opened the front door. There was an indescribable silence.

After Ben came through the doorway, that silence followed him inside. We just stood there in the lobby, staring at each other and frozen for several seconds. He wore a Polo sweater and a pair of Levis.

There he stood in the flesh, a handsome young man, same complexion and features as myself. I was simultaneously humbled and proud. I couldn't believe it.

He was a Butler, no doubt about it. I was staring at a male version of myself. Then we both exhaled. He finally broke the silence. "Well, give me a hug!" he said.

"OK," I said.

It was one of the happiest moments in my life.

I showed him around the center and then we chatted for about three hours. Then we drove over to the home of my niece, Deborah McKetty. It was such a wonderful family gathering. Everybody wanted to hug him and were just awe-struck about how much my son and I look like.

I was in La La Land. I couldn't believe this was happening. But it was and only by the grace of God. There was no way in the world I or anyone could have orchestrated this reunion the way God did.

*****

I got another surprise involving my son. It took place a few months after we met in December 2012. He returned March 2013 to attend the Women Making History event, an annual fundraiser for the Greenville Cultural Exchange Center. He surprised me by presenting me with a lovely bouquet of flowers at the end of the event.

Usually at the end, a committee member will present me with flowers in appreciation. The committee planned this without my knowledge of course.

I didn't know that my son would be the one who would deliver that evening. It was a very happy and proud moment in my life although I chuckle at the reaction of some folks when they found out I had a son.

"We are going to have Mr. Brown present his mother with flowers," said Marcia Williams, chairperson for the Women Making History committee. "Will Ruth Ann Butler please come up?"

The closer I got to the podium, mouths dropped. When we were on stage standing next to each other, I heard several camera clicks. So many people knew me for years but never knew about that part of my life which I so quietly and carefully guarded until that moment.

## Chapter 11: Women Making History

W omen Making History started as a fundraiser but became so much more. It is an event that is near and dear to my heart because of those we honor. Over the years, we have acknowledged local women in the fields of business, education, politics, the arts and community service. These are everyday women doing extraordinary things in the community.

*Ruth Ann Butler with former Women Making History*
*Chairman David Gray*

My friend, Linda Graden Murray, suggested that a committee be formed for some fundraising ideas for the center. So Murray looked through my address book and selected a group of people from the community to invite for one brainstorming session. That session involved different small groups and we narrowed our ideas down to one main concept: We would do something to honor and celebrate women. We decided it would be held in March, Women's History Month.

My niece, Deborah McKetty, was instrumental in setting this up. She initiated research and discovered that there was really nothing on a community-wide level that celebrated women in the Upstate during the month of March.

*Women Making History Chairperson Marcia Williams with committee member Pearlie Harris*

*Here I am with friend and supporter Joe Erwin at the 2016 Women Making History Awards. *Photo courtesy of Margaret Rose Media, LLC.*

McKetty was the chairperson for the first few years and orchestrated everything from setting up sponsorships and booking the venue to getting a logo and establishing criteria for award nominations.

The first event took place in 2005 at The Embassy Suites on Verdae Boulevard. We honored 11 women. We were impressed and pleasantly surprised with how well it was received by the Greenville community. Since our inception, 69 women have been recognized.

David Gray, former City of Greenville employee, took the reins as chairperson after Deborah stepped down. When Gray stepped down, Motivational Speaker, Trainer and Coach Marcia Williams, became chairperson. I am so grateful for these and others who so diligently served on the committee.

Women Making History has been going strong for 12 years. It has indeed been a privilege to highlight local women of diverse skills and backgrounds. Every year, we celebrate inspiring stories of trials, tribulations, victories and achievements. Hopefully, this annual recognition will motivate others to work hard, achieve their potential and serve their community.

*Ruth Ann Butler with friend and supporter Frankie Felder at the 2016 Women Making History Awards.*
*\*Photo courtesy of Margaret Rose Media, LLC.*

*2013 Women Making History Awards Committee: Top (from left to right): Rory Griffin, Helen Pinson, Lisa Uldrick, Josh Edgar, Dr. Grady Butler, Linda Sullivan and Glenn Williams; Bottom (from left to right): Glenis Redmond, Daisy Booker, Ruth Ann Butler and Marcia Williams*

## Chapter 12: Research & Reconciliation

From a Biblical standpoint, I believe all evil committed in this world stems from sin—no matter the skin color of the culprits. The history of mankind is filled with stories of tragedies as well as triumphs.

It's not always good to dwell in the past. However, it is crucial to acknowledge and learn from it. As far as African and African-American history is concerned, there are some things that many folks continue to deny or dilute.

Many Southerners, for instance, may trivialize the legacy and long-lasting impact of African slavery by denying little or any connection to the Confederacy.

Africans were stolen from their land, sold as objects and treated like animals. Stripped of their culture, dignity and names, they were not even considered humans. Still Africa is a symbol of resilience because despite genocide, resource exploitation, theft and corruption, her descendants are all over the world surviving and thriving.

*Joint Forces: Several local leaders worked together to bring the story of Willie Earle to light. Earle was kidnapped from a Pickens jail and was lynched by a white mob after being accused of killing a white taxi cab driver.*

Americans of African descent have come a long way but there is still work to be done. Sometimes when "progress" happens, we easily forget the past struggles leading up to those changes. So we downplay or trivialize history's dark side. And when that takes place, we become incapable of reconciliation, thus perpetuating the same cycle of problems for future generations.

For instance, the same folks who want to bury America's racist past perpetuate racism by not coming to terms with eras and tragic events that adversely affected generations.

What's the point if we haven't acquired any understanding, wisdom or reconciliation from the past? It's ok to question the answers, to analyze, discuss, share and even contemplate your role in the overall scheme of things. Researching history should produce benefits and results.

When you do research, make sure you ask yourself: "Why am I doing this? What exactly am I learning and how can I use this information to educate and improve the lives of others?

A lot of black history has been passed down from generation to generation orally because for a long time, we were not allowed to read and write. Also many textbooks have omitted black history. On top of this, colonialism and slavery have instilled in us a feeling of shame and to some degree, confusion about our heritage.

As a researcher, I continue to pursue avenues for the public to have access to black history.

When it comes to racism in the American South, we can ask all sorts of questions all day long about the injustices that took place including segregation, brutal lynchings of innocent black men, women and children and Jim Crow laws that ignited the Civil Rights Movement.

Two well-documented cases come to mind regarding the racism and abuse of Black Americans in the South: Emmett Till of Mississippi and Willie Earle in South Carolina.

\*\*\*\*\*

I never expected a conversation with Greenville County Councilwoman Xanthene Norris to snowball into what it did.

In 2006, Norris received a phone call from a former student whom she taught at Sterling High School. This former student knew of a gentleman who was involved in a Mississippi project designed to increase awareness and attention to the gruesome case of Emmett Till. Till was a black Mississippi teenager who in 1955 was brutally beaten and shot by white men for allegedly flirting with a white woman.

Apparently, this gentleman in Mississippi heard about the Willie Earle case in South Carolina and wanted to join forces with folks from the Upstate.

Willie Earle, a black man was accused of killing a white taxi cab driver. The incident allegedly took place in Greenville but Earle was thrown in a Pickens County jail. A mob of malicious and armed white men (mainly cab drivers) snatched Earle from the jail in Pickens, brutally lynched him and left his body remains off U.S. 124 near Old Bramlett Road. This was supposedly South Carolina's last lynching.

There were similarities between the two cases, so the Till Commission in Mississippi wanted to pick our brains and get ideas that might help further their efforts.

After Mrs. Norris spoke with Mississippi officials, she approached me about traveling to Mississippi so that we could gain insight for a few local projects she wanted to pursue. Those projects included setting up a guided tour, publishing a booklet and establishing historical markers in remembrance of Willie Earle.

Committee members for this mission comprised several local leaders and residents including retired educator Ruth M. Richburg, businessman Andre Richburg, attorney and activist Efia Nwangaza, Greenville County Councilwoman Xanthene Norris, Dr. Grady Butler, Edith Chou, college professor and author Dr. Will Gravely, South Carolina Senator Karl Allen, Judy Benedict, Tara Davis, Rev. Sean Dogan, County Councilwoman Lottie B. Gibson, Rev. Terry King, Joan Peters, Russell Stall and Dr. Baxter Wynn.

Local media including Greenville News writer Richard E. Walton and TV reporter Nigel Robertson from Channel 4, traveled to Mississippi to cover the story.

We stayed there approximately three days and during that time, we met with Mississippi officials and local press. By the third day, we had national media attention.

Within a year, we returned to Mississippi and were able to witness the achievements of the Till Commission. Our group decided we needed to do the same in honor of Willie Earle. It took a few years but through the grace of God, we got it done.

We solicited and received donations for the funding of a booklet detailing the events of the Willie Earle Lynching and two markers. One marker was placed behind City Hall which is where the old courthouse was and another on Old Bramlett Road, (off Pendleton Street) that was the location for the field where Earle's body was found.

City of Greenville officials refused to allow the committee to put a marker on Main Street. The marker on Old Bramlett Road has since been torn down by vandals.

## Chapter 13: Richland Cemetery

The Richland Cemetery was another important research project I was involved in. The cemetery sits on a small hill located on Sunflower Street, just off East Stone Avenue in Greenville.

I was contacted by then City of Greenville Councilwomen Chandra Dillard and Diane Smock in regard to this cemetery. The city owned the property but nobody knew the history of it. They were very interested in finding out about Richland Cemetery. They hired me to research it.

It was during the month of July and I documented names and information on tombstones and put the data in alphabetical order according to the section in which they were buried. This took a couple of months and I didn't have a computer. I was out there every day for several hours.

Two sisters, Elizabeth and Emmala Jones owned that property. They were matrons at the Anne Cigar Company. In 1884, the sisters sold the cemetery to the City of Greenville for the use of the burial of African-Americans.

When I first arrived, the grounds were unkempt. Some of the markers were out of place. City officials were under the impression that Richland was sort of a pauper's graveyard. But in doing my research, I discovered it was just the opposite.

I discovered many of the buried were pioneers of Greenville: Hattie Logan Duckett who started the Phillis Wheatley Center, Rev. D.M. Minus who started Sterling High School, Cora Chapman, one of the first black nurses in Greenville, as well as black doctors, dentists, veterans and other professionals.

Mrs. Duckett was a mentor of mine so I was elated to discover her tombstone. It was exciting. This graveyard was yet another historical gem I came across.

I worked mornings into the afternoon until the sun became unbearable. It was in July so it was hot. I wore a hat and shades. I carried a little stool and clipboard. I created my own document to list and organized plot information. I did one plot at a time. I was methodical and focused, approaching one section at a time.

When I wasn't at the cemetery recording information with pencil and paper, I was at the museum on the telephone tracking and interviewing descendants. I was a woman on a mission and I thoroughly enjoyed it. I still have the original notes I wrote. I found myself writing the history as well as a report.

I documented more than 700 plots. Each section was documented in alphabetical order. The oldest person documented there was buried in 1884. I am still in the process of documenting people.

When I finished, the City of Greenville posted the history of The Richland Cemetery on its website--written by Ruth Ann Butler, Greenville Cultural Exchange Center. As a result, the Richland Cemetery was listed on the National Register of Historic Places in October 2005. It was among the first cemeteries in the Upstate to be listed as such.

The late Cheryl Ratliff, a dear friend of mine who was a clerk for the City of Greenville, helped me gather all the names and contact information of the descendants of the people buried there. We formed a group called Friends of The Richland Cemetery.

From that, the city formed a board of trustees for The Richland Cemetery. The board started an annual veteran's memorial service at the cemetery honoring local black veterans. Every November, descendants and the public are invited.

## Chapter 14: The gift of research

Research is one of the best gifts of all time. It is so much fun. I'm right at home in the library. I'm addicted to learning. I live and breathe facts, eras, dates, places, faces, people and events.

But please have no doubt about this---it can be time consuming and grueling!  Just because you love to do something doesn't mean that it's always easy to do.

The adrenalin is something else.  Once you get me going on a project, there's no turning back.  There have been plenty of times when I've stayed up until 4 or 5 in the morning, looking over photos, articles, documents and surfing the web.

My advice: Be diligent and persistent about your research.  Have purpose. Strategize. Engage yourself. Indulge in the why. Again, question the answers. Analyze.  See what your role is in the overall scheme of things.  Make sure you're in it for the long haul.  It's more than just a term paper or a homework assignment.  And while the Internet and Google are awesome resources, research is more than just typing key words and clicking on websites.

Successful research comes in increments. Sometimes you have more questions than answers. If you get overwhelmed, take a break.  Research is like an awesome puzzle of sorts and when that puzzle is complete, you can step back and enjoy the fruits of your labor. Plus, you get to share that fruit with others.

There are many genealogy websites and software programs that are helpful. For instance, Ancestry.com and Findagrave.com are two sites I frequently use. Dig deep with online archives, public government records and microfilm. And don't discount the old-fashioned telephone interview. Don't take anything for granted. Gather as much information as you can. You may not need all the data you collect but at least, you have enough to select what you need.

Even if you're not a researcher at heart, there's a detective aspect that's quite thrilling and rewarding.

You can discover so much exciting and wonderful stuff about your family, your community and the world. You get a global

insight about people, places, events and time periods.

I've always loved history. I didn't realize my calling for research until after I stopped teaching. That calling became clearer as more people would contact me to help them find information—from long lost ancestors to events that took place in Greenville. For instance, one man came to me who could not find his family on the US Census. He had a French last name. So I asked him for first names and was able to locate his family each year on the US Census. We discovered that each time, the last name was spelled differently but it was the same family.

I became enthused with each inquiry and once I found what I was looking for, I had an incredible sense of accomplishment. I simply loved the challenge of digging up information. Today, I get several requests a year from all over the country.

\*\*\*\*\*

I started researching information via microfiche. This was in the '70s. You could find the census but it did not index names. You just had to scroll until you found what you were looking for.

Prior to my resignation from teaching, I never worked on a computer.

The two things that really impressed me about computers were that you were able to name and file documents, and you could correct something as you go. I was ready to work even harder using this technology.

When attorney Robert Jenkins hired me to work for Legal Services, (this was prior to him becoming a judge) he asked if I ever worked on a computer. I said, yes. I figured a computer wasn't that much different from a typewriter. I never took a typing lesson and I taught myself to work the typewriter. Indeed, there were similarities but I soon found out working on a computer was different and took some figuring out.

I found it a bit challenging doing mail merge as I had to mail up to 500 letters and I had to publish a newsletter every month. I stored a lot of information on a floppy disc.

Whatever I didn't know, I asked one of the secretaries at Legal Services. They demonstrated and then I would run back to my desk and practice. One of the greatest gifts and skills you can possess is having the courage to say you don't know. I had no problem asking questions and I was grateful for the secretaries' willingness to help. I applied whatever I learned at the agency to my position at the Greenville Cultural Exchange Center.

Nobody told me how to research, run a business or start a museum. A little "TLC "(trial, error and correction) was a personal motto of mine.

I remember the first computer I owned. Someone graciously donated a Hewlett-Packard to the Greenville Cultural Exchange Center. I was determined to build my computer and typing skills. Sometimes, I would stay up until 2 or 3 in the morning working on that device.

Today, this piece of technology is now a piece of history in itself as it is still housed at the center. That computer also serves as yet another personal reminder of what I've overcome despite my physical disability.

I may have stopped teaching but I didn't cease learning. My thirst for knowledge never quenched. I learned all that I could about computers, history, running a business, office management and whatever other pertinent information my brain could soak up. Experiences beyond the classroom helped me discover my true passion. I love history. I am a researcher. It's what I do. It's who I am. It's who I always will be.

*Photo courtesy of Margaret Rose Media, LLC.*

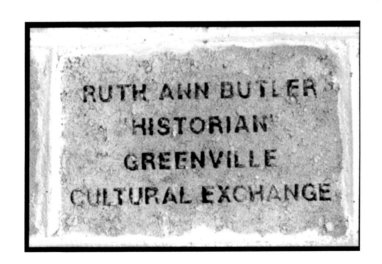

## ACKNOWLEDGEMENTS:

I want to first and foremost acknowledge my Lord and Personal Savior Jesus Christ, for without him, none of this would be possible.

This is probably one of the most challenging sections of my book since God has blessed me through so many people. I can't list everyone in print but in my heart, I leave no one out.

I want to express my loving gratitude to my family whose support has been immeasurable throughout my journey. I want to thank my parents who have gone to be with the Lord. I treasured them for being Christ-like role models and wisely utilizing their God-given talents.

I want to thank my son, Benjamin, for stepping up and stepping in when he did. I'm so humbled that he is a part of my life. I love him dearly. Hugs and kisses to my daughter-n-law, Alison and my beautiful grandchildren, Mia (aka "Baby Ruth") and Aiden.

Thumbs up to The Greenville News for seeing the value of writing about the Greenville Cultural Exchange Center over the years. Thanks to Margaret Rose Media LLC for helping me to edit this book.

From the bottom of my heart, I thank all of those who have volunteered and served on the board for the Greenville Cultural Exchange Center and on the committee for the center's annual Women Making History Awards, individual and corporate donors, participating organizations and of course, my church family at Allen Temple AME in Downtown Greenville.

To all who have played a role (big or small), I offer you my deepest sincerity and gratitude.

Once again, I thank God. It all begins and ends with HIM.......

*Ruth Ann Butler*

*"Seek ye first the Kingdom of God, and His righteousness; and all these things shall be added unto you."* **Matthew 6:33**

*"I can do everything through Christ who strengthens me."* **Philippians 4:13**

*"Do not be anxious about anything but in everything, by prayer and petition, with thanksgiving, present your requests to God. And the peace of God, which transcends all understanding, will guard your hearts and your minds in Christ Jesus."* **Philippians 4:6-7**

*"For I know the plans I have for you, thoughts of peace and not evil...."* **Jeremiah 29:11**

*"Being confident of this, that He who began a good work in you will carry it onto completion until the day of Christ Jesus."* **Philippians 1:6**

*"And we know that all things work together for the good of them that love God to them who are called according to His purpose."* **Romans 8:28**

# About the Author

Ruth Ann Butler is the Founder and Executive Director of the Greenville Cultural Exchange Center, a museum dedicated exclusively to promoting the history and contributions of African Americans in Upstate South Carolina.

She has dedicated much of her life to teaching, researching and sharing.

Ruth is the ninth child of the late Baptist minister Rev. C. E. and Mrs. Butler. A native of Greenville, SC, Ruth is a proud alumni of Sterling High School and Benedict College. She taught in the public school system for several years and as an independent researcher, taught genealogy workshops for the Greenville County Library System. She also contributed to research projects for the City of Greenville, Greenville County, local churches and organizations.

Ruth is an avid reader, learner, researcher, storyteller and community activist. She is an endearing mom, sister, aunt and grandmother of two.

Writing this memoir was a bucket list item she has dreamed about for quite some time.

Made in the USA
Columbia, SC
15 May 2017